Kai to the Rescue!

For Buzz, who enriches us with tall tales — A.P.

ISBN: 978-1-338-13016-4

10 9 8 7 6 5 4 3 2   16 17 18 19 20

Printed in the U.S.A   40
First printing 2016
The illustrations were created digitally.

Book design by Steve Ponzo

Kai to the Rescue!

by **AUDREY PENN** illustrated by **MIKE YAMADA**

Scholastic Inc.

Once upon a time, there were three red fire trucks who lived at Firehouse #10.

Chuck, the large hook and ladder, was captain of the firehouse. He was very proud of his long ladder, which could reach to the top of the highest flames.

Emily, the equipment truck, carried fire-fighting tools like axes and air tanks so everyone could breathe clean air.

And **Rudy**, the big chemical pumper truck, carried foam to fill the hoses.

Every night when the lights went out, the three fire trucks stood side by side by side, clean and polished, ready for the next day's action.

One day, Captain Chuck received word that a brand-new pumper truck named Kai was coming to work at Firehouse #10.

"Oh, no, no, no!" wailed the captain. *"This will not do! I'm very happy with my crew, crew, crew!"*

But, later that night, when the trucks were almost asleep,
the bay doors opened and Kai rolled into the darkened garage.

Captain Chuck reached across the room with his longest fire hose and flipped on the light switch with the nozzle.

There, in the middle of the engine room, stood a very little,
very nervous, very shy pumper truck, gleaming in green and white!

All three firehouse trucks turned on their headlights and stared down at poor little Kai. Suddenly, the large hook and ladder sputtered.

"Good gracious, Kai! You're so young and small!
I really don't think you can help us at all. And look at that paint job!
Fire trucks are red! You just won't do, like I said, said, said."

The little pumper truck tried not to cry.
"I'm a very good firefighter," he told the captain. "You'll see."

"Well, I think green and white are lovely," said Emily.
"Me, too," boomed Rudy. The voice of the large pumper truck echoed in a deep, vibrating tone and Kai jumped.
"Thank you." His little bell jingled.

That night, while the three big fire trucks slept, the nervous little pumper peeked around the engine room in the spill of the soft yellow night-light. There, on a table across the room, sat a basketful of red crayons used by visiting children.

"I have an idea!" thought Kai. He quietly unwound his longest fire hose and inched it across the firehouse floor. When it reached the table, he lifted the basket of crayons with the nozzle and carried it back to his green-and-white truck.

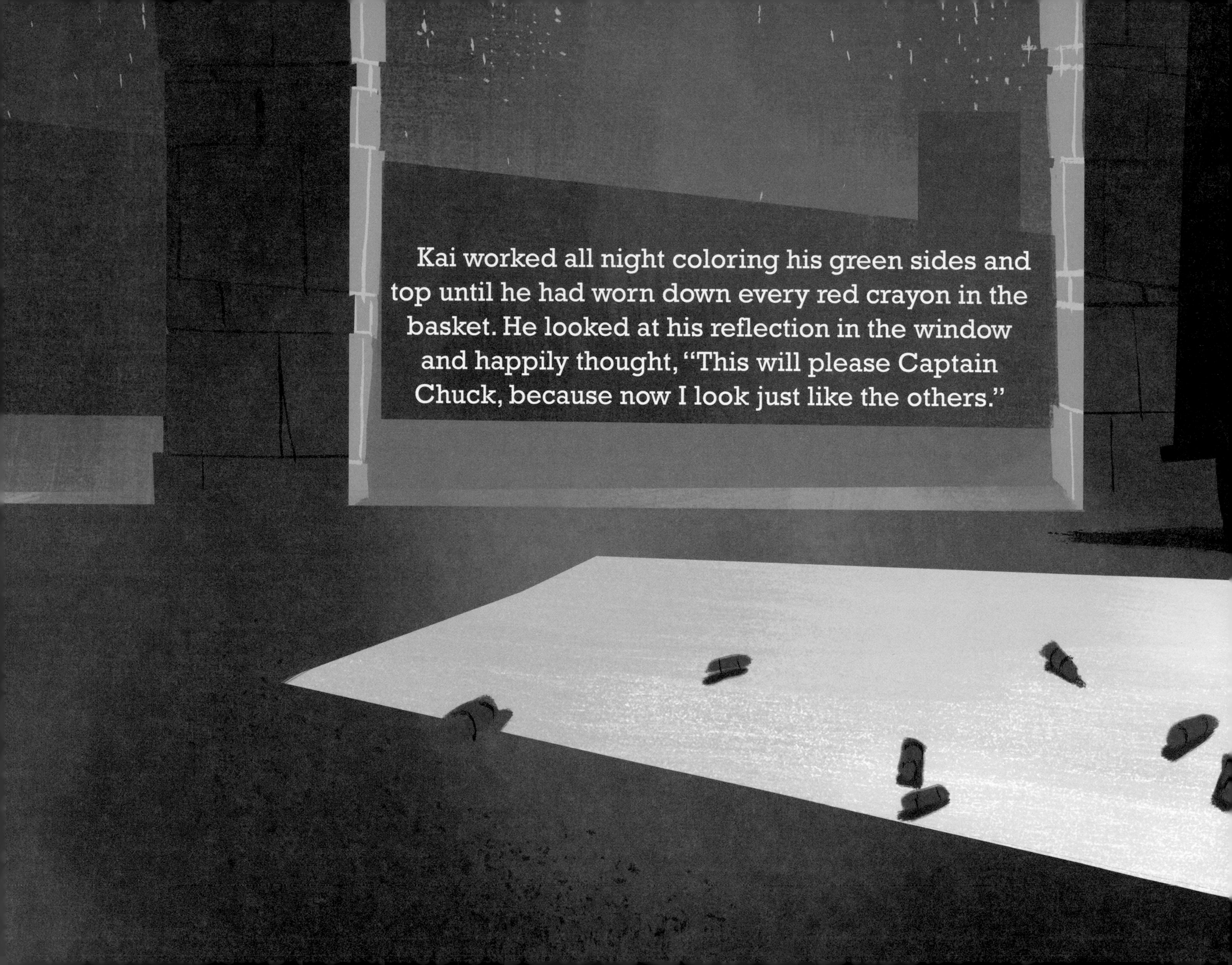

Kai worked all night coloring his green sides and top until he had worn down every red crayon in the basket. He looked at his reflection in the window and happily thought, "This will please Captain Chuck, because now I look just like the others."

Early the next morning, the fire alarm clanged at Firehouse #10.
All four trucks roared to life as the bay doors opened.

"Wow! Good coloring!" tooted the equipment truck as Kai drove into the street.
"Very stylish!" vroomed the great big pumper.

"Kai!" yelled the captain. *"I can't believe my eyes. You've turned yourself red! What a surprise! But underneath that crayon you're still white and green. I don't think you're right for our team, team, team."*

The large hook and ladder turned on his siren and drove ahead of the little pumper.

A few minutes later the four trucks arrived at the forest fire. Captain Chuck quickly raised his ladder while directing the other large trucks where to go and what to do.

"Listen up!" hailed the captain. *"Stay safe! Watch your truck. Let's put out this fire. Good luck, luck, luck."*

Emily quickly cleared a path through the woods for Rudy. The great big pumper truck filled his hoses and showered the flames with thick, white foam.

"How about me?" Kai called to the captain. "I want to help!"
Captain Chuck stared down at the little pumper.

"Move away from the heat. Keep clear of the flame.
Fighting fire is dangerous — not a game, game, game."

"All right," sighed Kai. He was very disappointed,
but he did as he was told.

Kai rolled to the curb and parked. From a distance, he watched and learned as the large hook and ladder, the equipment truck, and the great big pumper did their particular jobs, but together tamed the fire as a well-trained squad.

Suddenly, Kai noticed a small fire burning deep in the underbrush, out of the sight of the larger trucks. He quickly rang his bell and called for Captain Chuck.

The hook and ladder was very concerned.

"Our trucks won't fit in that underbrush. But we have a little pumper who's new. Kai, you're the truck who is right for the job. Are you ready to join our crew, crew, crew?"

“Yes!” cheered Kai. He quickly turned over his engine, then bravely crushed through sparking timber and low-hanging branches until he reached the flaming underbrush.

Kai pumped water through his fire hose with all his might. Sweat poured down his sides as heat from the fire melted away the red crayon. Kai was soon fire fighting as the green-and-white truck he truly was, and he suddenly felt very proud.

Captain Chuck was pleased and relieved as he watched Kai
put out the fire. The captain tooted his horn happily
when the little pumper came rolling out of the woods.

"Good work!" Emily rang.
"Very impressive!" Rudy boomed.
Trucks from every fire station lined up
to congratulate the new little pumper
for doing such a fine job.

"*It seems to me,*" said Captain Chuck,
"*I was wrong about green and white. You're a very good firefighter, Kai. I admit you were right, right, right.*"

"Red trucks don't work any harder than you. As you see, you fit in just fine. When the fire is out, we all look the same: the color of dirt, ash, and grime."

And so it was, that night, the new team of four trucks returned home to Firehouse #10.

Tired and ready for sleep, Chuck, Emily, Rudy, and Kai stood
side by side by side by side, clean and polished, and ready for action.

Suddenly,
Chuck began to sing:

"Kai is a pumper truck, green and white.
Kai fights fire with all his might.
Kai's not red, but he does his part.
He's a little pumper truck with a great big heart.
Hooray for Kai! Just watch him gleam!
We're lucky to have him on our team, team, team!

Go, Kai!
Go, Kai!"